# Morning!

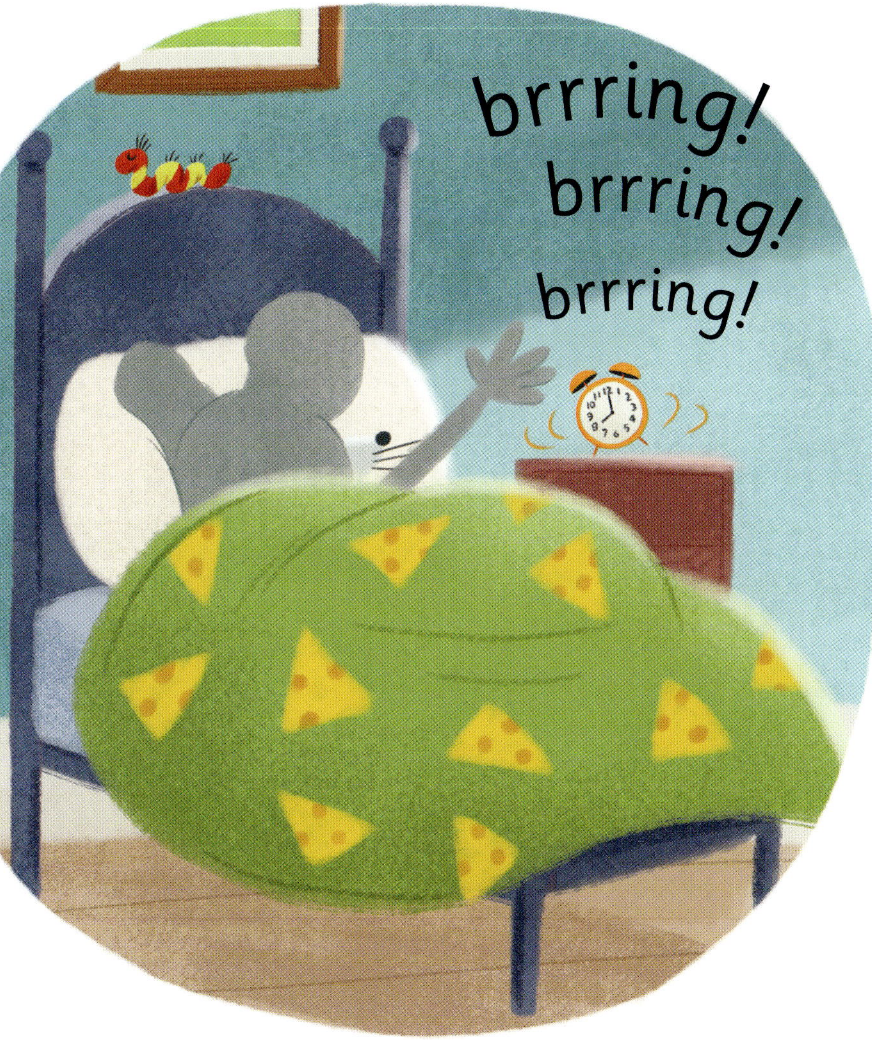

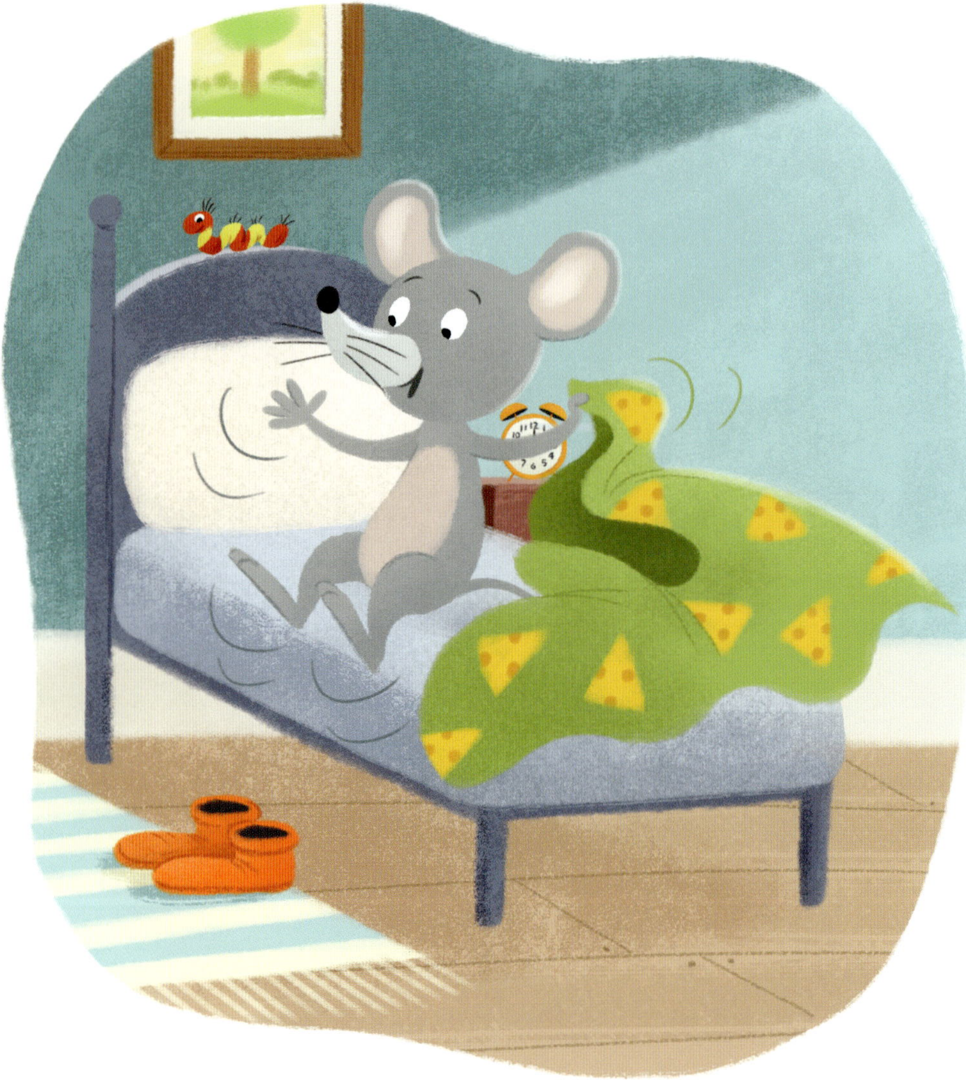

She gets up.

She dresses.

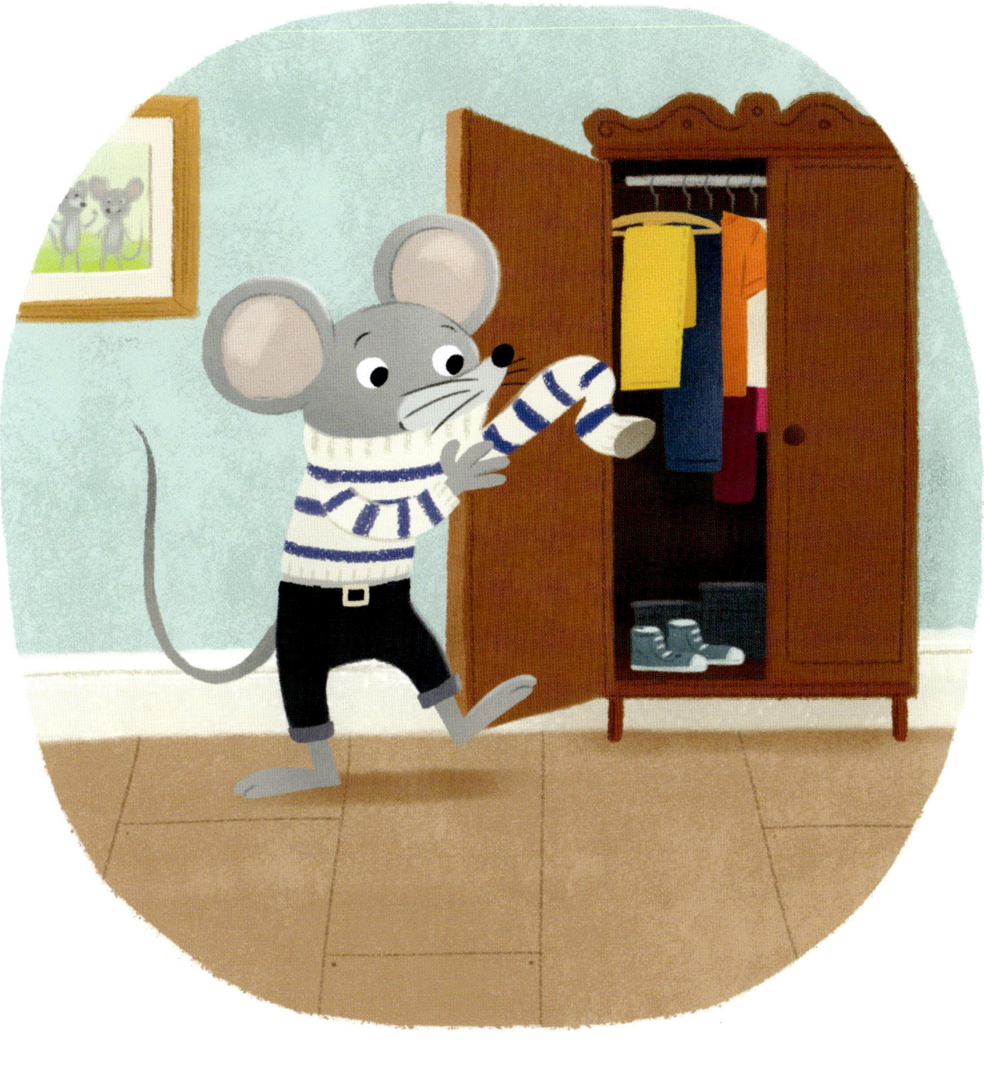

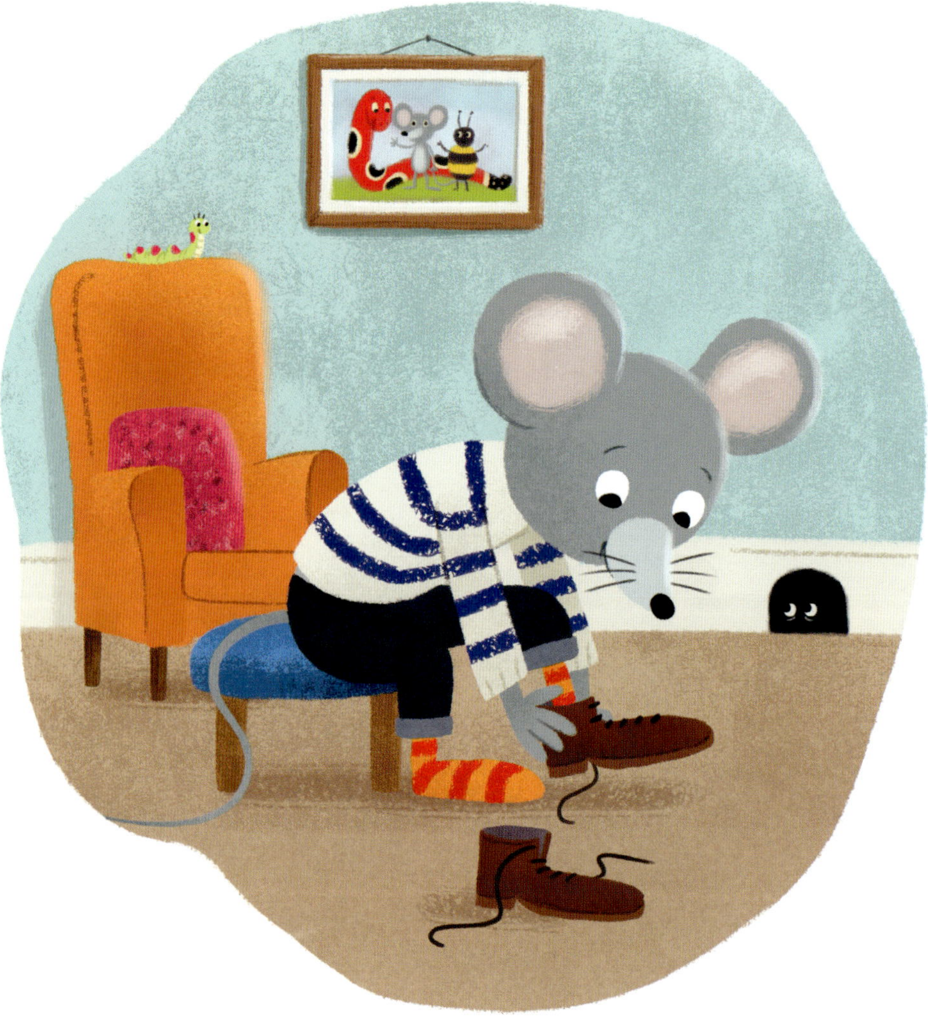

Socks and boots on...

hat and scarf
on...

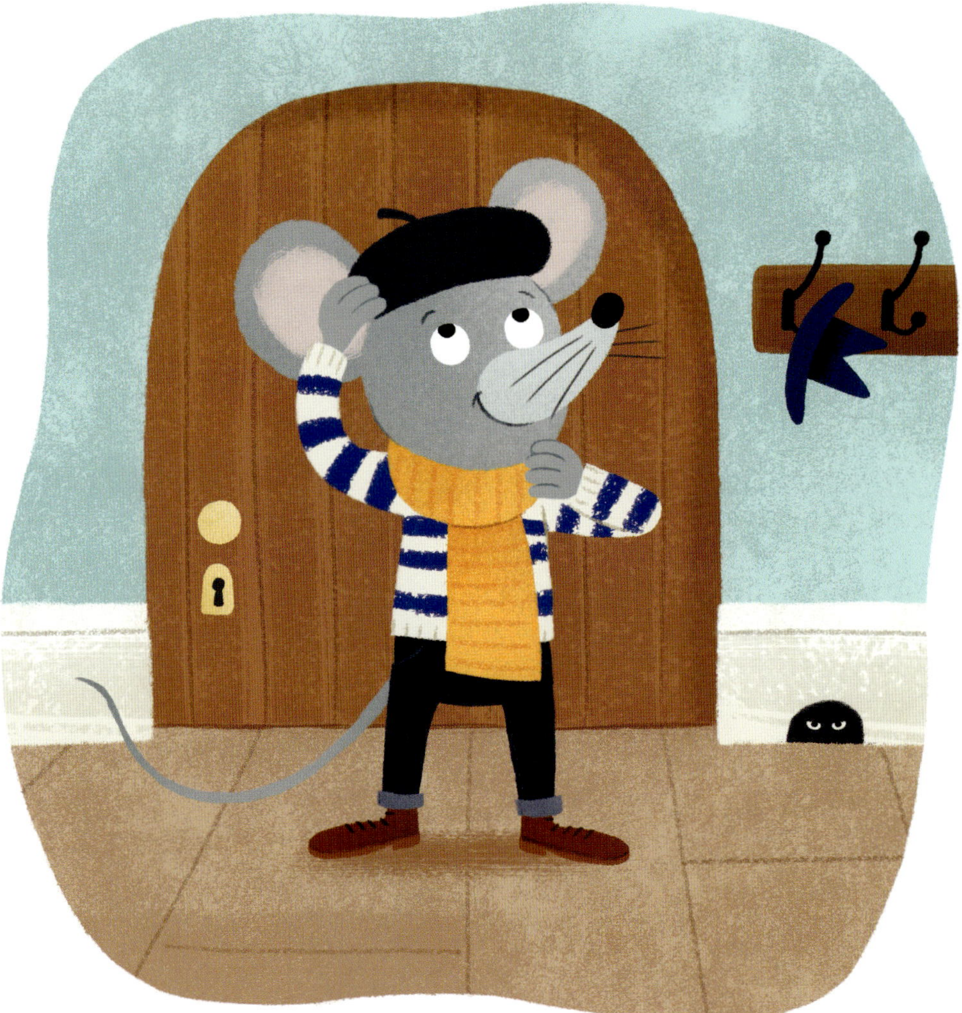

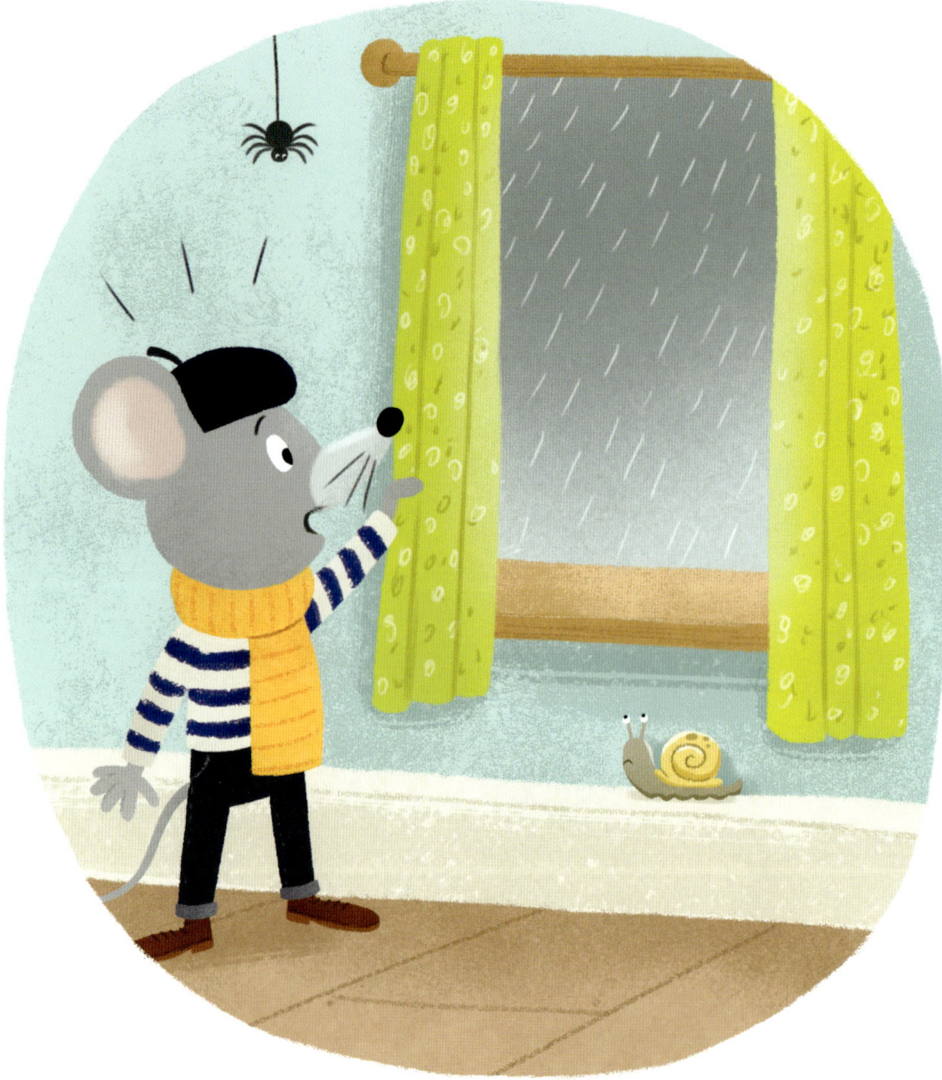

It's raining!

# Off with the lot...

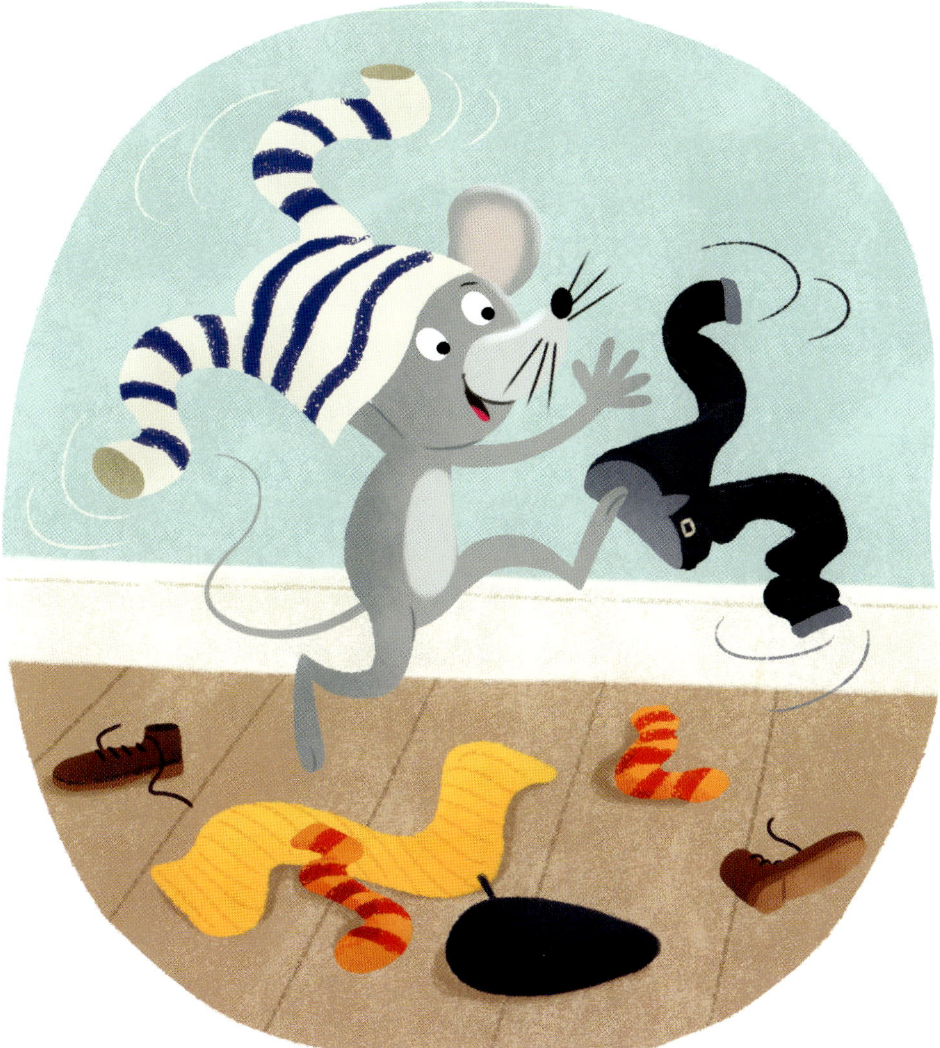

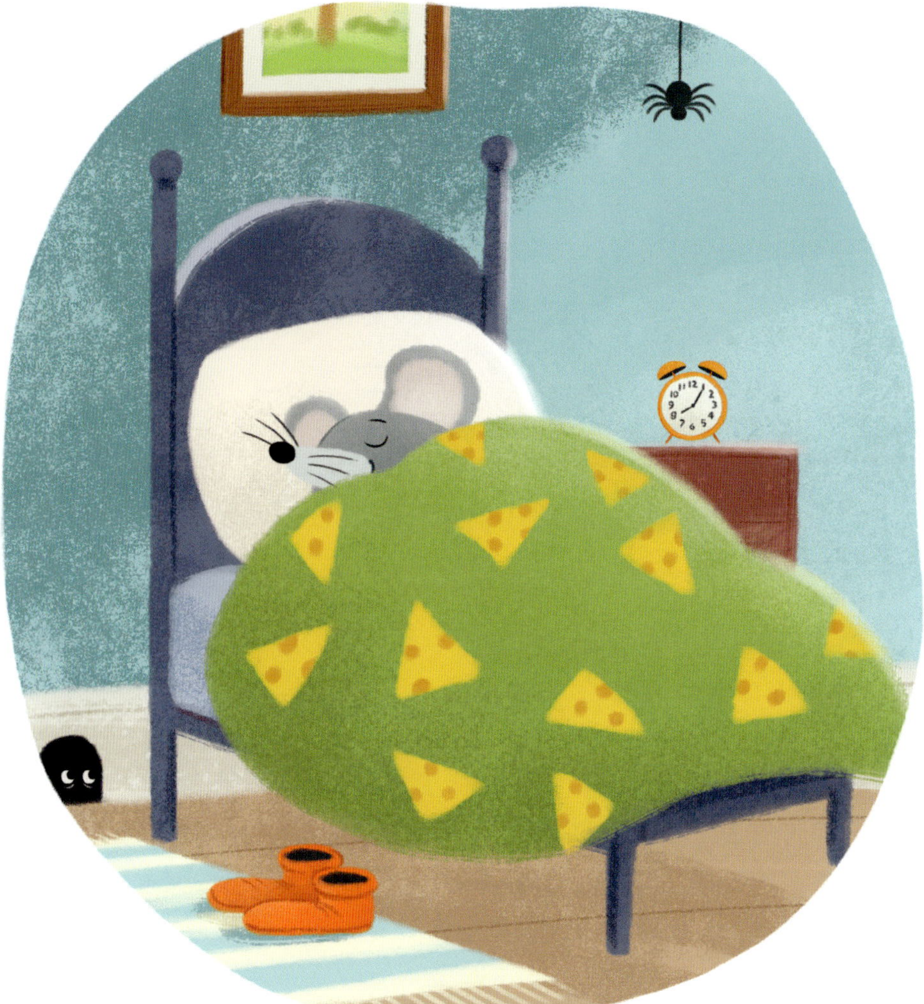

and back in bed!